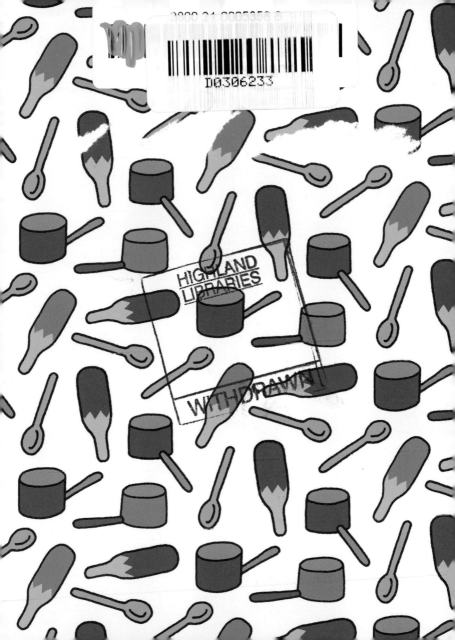

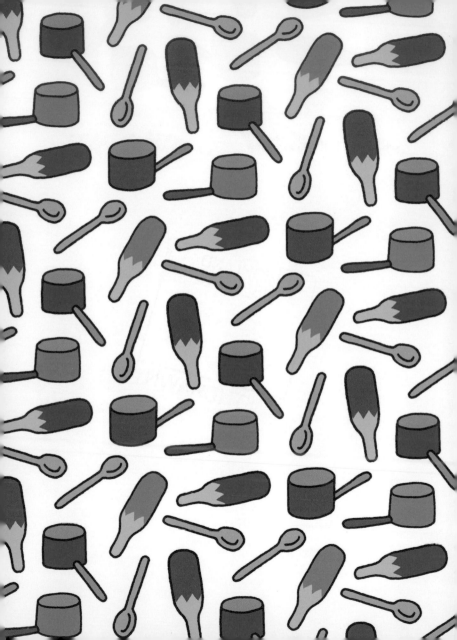

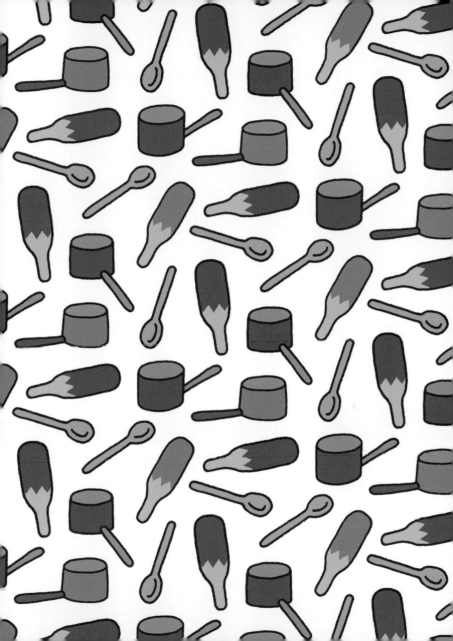

This book belongs to:

_____

Nick Sharratt

Tea Party Parade

Barrington Stoke

First published in 2021 in Great Britain by
Barrington Stoke Ltd
18 Walker Street, Edinburgh, EH3 7LP

www.barringtonstoke.co.uk

Text & Illustrations © 2021 Nick Sharratt

A CIP catalogue record for this book is available
from the British Library upon request

ISBN: 978-1-80090-001-1

Printed by Hussar Books, Poland

This book is in a super-readable format for young readers
beginning their independent reading journey.

This book is dedicated to
St Paul's C of E Primary School

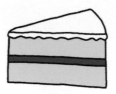

There's the most enormous teapot
in the playground.

1

There are great big cups and saucers
by the slide.

There's a giant jug of juice near
the bushes,

a jolly large jelly next to the fence

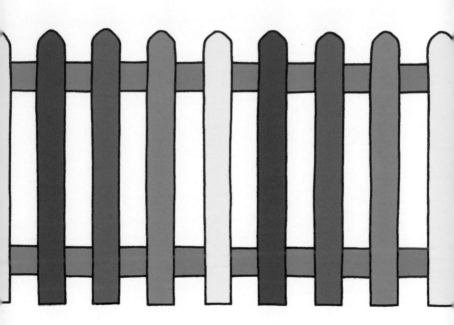

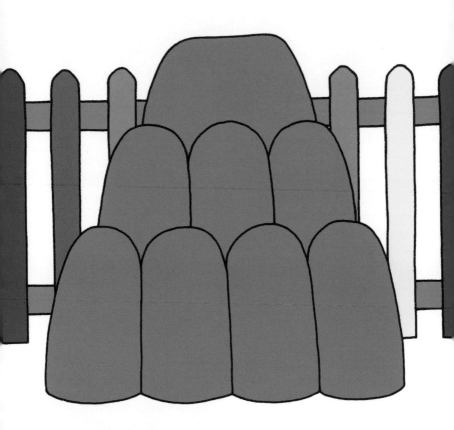

and jumbo jam tarts round the tree.

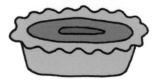

There are slices of cake on the hopscotch

and slabs of swiss roll in the goal.

WHAT'S GOING ON?

Well ... every Spring, on the first Saturday in May, the schools in the town have a

Children's Parade

This time it's Class One's turn to take part.

YESSSSSSSSSSS!!!!

It's all very exciting.

Class One have been busy making costumes (with a little bit of help from the grown-ups).

They've been planning

and sketching

and measuring

and tearing

and gluing

and cutting

and sewing

and stapling

and painting

and spraying

and stencilling.

Class One are dressing up as a
TEA PARTY!

And now it's time for an after-school parade practice.

Here comes Class One.

They find their groups
and help each other get
into their costumes.

Mr Flack,
Gabby,
William,
Soraya,
Lucy,
Freya,
Jason
and Todd

are the Jam Tart Squad.

Michael,

Preena,

Scarlett,

Stanley,

Dev

and Prue

are the Tea Cup Crew.

Oliver,

Amelie,

Abdullah,

Grace,

Tomas,

Tallulah,

Summer

and Cole

are Team Swiss Roll.

Tilly,

Benjie,

Christopher,

Rose,

Gina,

Toby,

Marcus

and Ann

are the

Sponge Cake Gang.

Mrs Bruce is the jug of juice.

Miss Kelly is the jelly.

And Mr Stott is the big teapot.

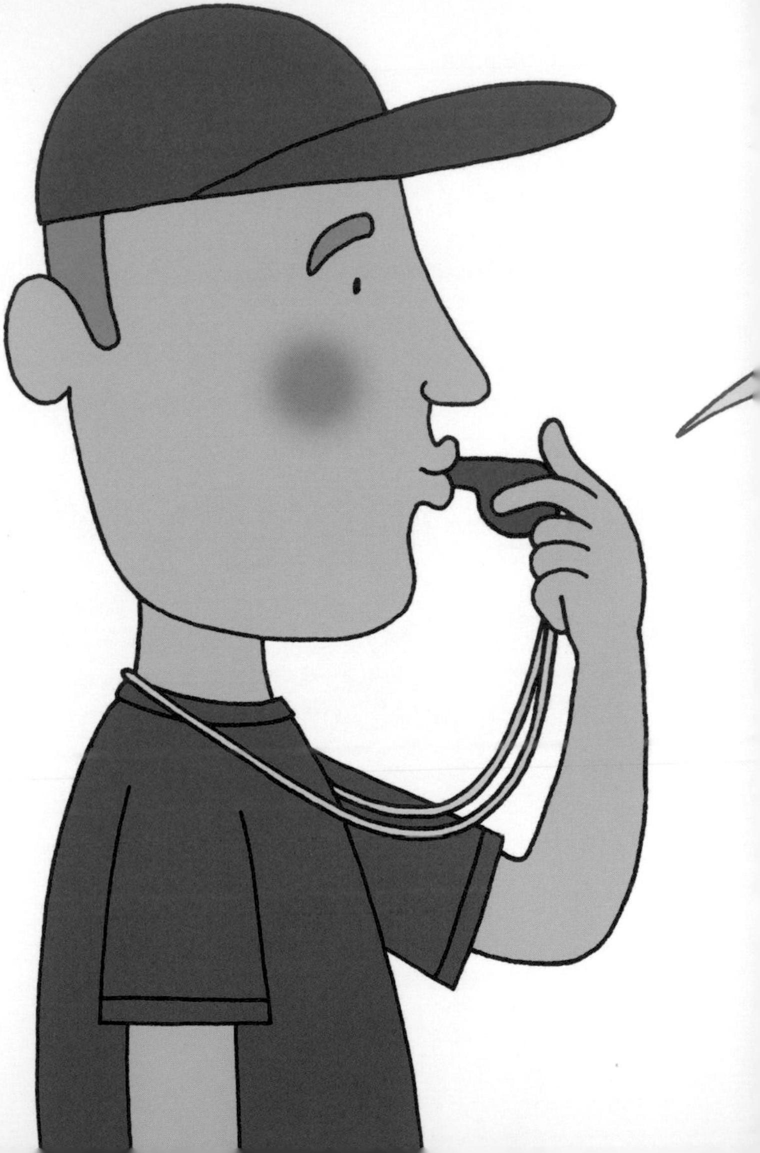

Mr Flack blows his whistle.

PEEEEEEEEEEEP!

and everyone gets into position.

He shouts,

"Ready, steady, GO!"

and they're off.

The jam tarts head off across
the playground.

They bang their drums and
shake their maracas.

Bang bang bang!

Rattle rattle rattle!

The teacups follow.

Each time Mr Stott shouts,

"Time for tea!" ...

the teacups run right round him.

Team Swiss Roll and the jelly come next.

Each time Miss Kelly shouts,

"Roly poly!" ...

the Swiss rolls form a line.

The Sponge Cake Gang
and the jug of juice
bring up the rear.

43

Each time Mrs Bruce shouts,

"Icing on the cake!" ...

the slices make
a circle.

Class One parades

this way and that way

and this way

and that way

until,

PEEEEEEEEEEEP!

Mr Flack blows his whistle.

"Good job, everyone," he says.
"Now we're all set for the parade.
Give yourselves a cheer."

And they do!

HIP HIP

HOORAY!

Class One get out of their costumes and
are just about to go home when,

PEEEEEEEEEEP!

It's Mr Flack again.

"Just before you leave," he says, "we've
got something for you."

Into the playground come Mrs Rose,

Mrs Mapp, Mr Ling and Miss Caldicott.

And look what they've got!

HIP HIP

HOORAY!

And roll on Saturday!

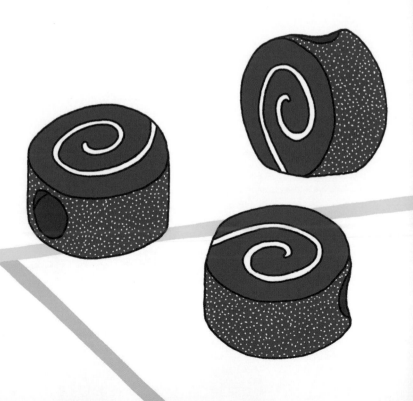

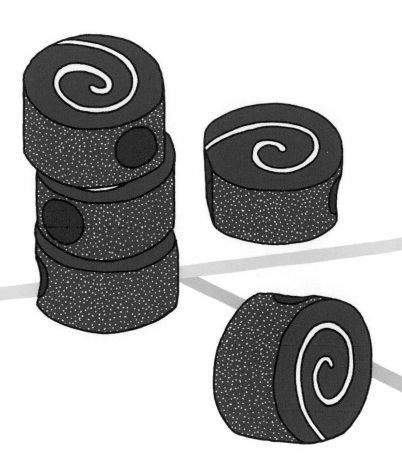

This book was inspired by the author's memory of seeing children in a school playground dressed as slices of cake.

They were getting ready for the much-loved Children's Parade, produced by Same Sky, which marks the official opening of the amazing Brighton Festival every May.

Our books are tested
for children and young people by
children and young people.

Thanks to everyone who consulted on
a manuscript for their time and effort in
helping us to make our books better
for our readers.

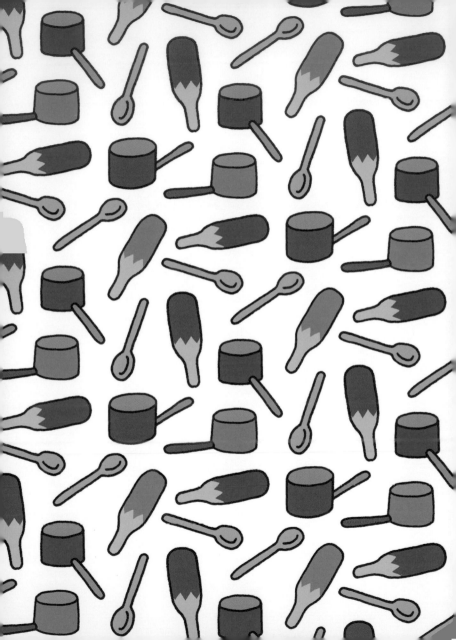

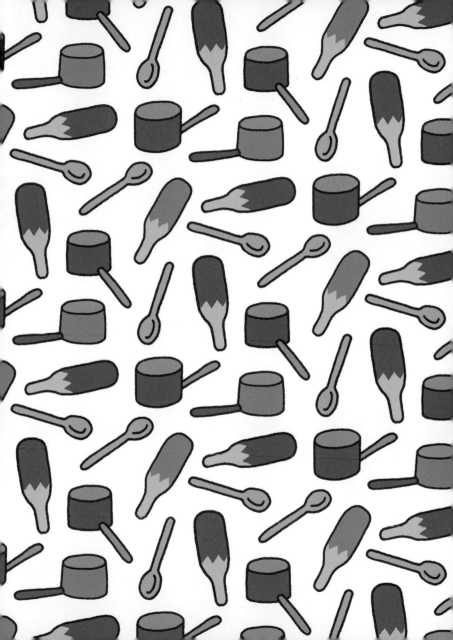